Dear Parents and Teachers,

In an easy-reader format, **My Readers** introduce classic stories to children who are learning to read. Although favorite characters and time-tested tales are the basis for **My Readers**, the books tell completely new stories and are freshly and beautifully illustrated.

My Readers are available in three levels:

 Level One is for the emergent reader and features repetitive language and word clues in the illustrations.

 Level Two is for more advanced readers who still need support saying and understanding some words. Stories are longer with word clues in the illustrations.

Level Three is for independent, fluent readers who enjoy working out occasional unfamiliar words. The stories are longer and divided into chapters.

Encourage children to select books based on interests, not reading levels. Read aloud with children, showing them how to use the illustrations for clues. With adult guidance and rereading, children will eventually read the desired book on their own.

Here are some ways you might want to use this book with children:

- Talk about the title and the cover illustrations. Encourage the child to use these to predict what the story is about.
- Discuss the interior illustrations and try to piece together a story based on the pictures. Does the child want to change or adjust his first prediction?
- After children reread a story, suggest they retell or act out a favorite part.

My Readers will not only help children become readers, they will serve as an introduction to some of the finest classic children's books available today.

—LAURA ROBB
Educator and Reading Consultant

For activities and reading tips, visit myreadersonline.com.

SQUARE
FISH

An Imprint of Macmillan Children's Publishing Group

Library of Congress Cataloging-in-Publication Data
Day, Alexandra.
Carl and the sick puppy / story and pictures by Alexandra Day. — 1st ed.
p. cm.
Summary: Carl tends to a sick puppy while the puppy's father takes the rest of his babies for a walk.
[1. Sick—Fiction. 2. Dogs—Fiction. 3. Animals—Infancy—Fiction.] I. Title.
PZ7.D32915Cao 2012   [E]—dc23   2011030861

ISBN 978-1-250-00152-8 (hardcover)
1   3   5   7   9   10   8   6   4   2

ISBN 978-1-250-00153-5 (paperback)
1   3   5   7   9   10   8   6   4   2

Book design by Patrick Collins/Véronique Lefèvre Sweet

Square Fish logo designed by Filomena Tuosto

First Edition: 2012

myreadersonline.com
mackids.com

This is a Level 1 book

LEXILE: 210L

CARL and the
SICK PUPPY

WITHDRAWN

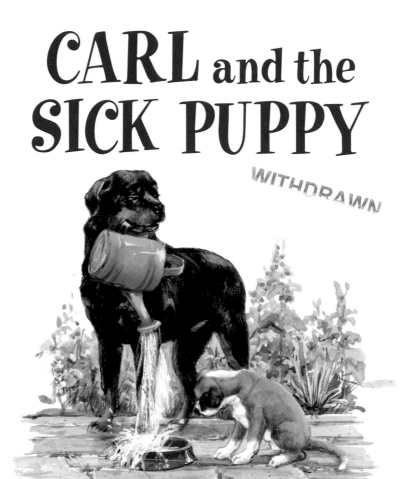

story and pictures by
Alexandra Day

SQUARE
FISH

Macmillan Children's Publishing Group
New York

One of Carl's friends
needs help.
Who can it be?

It's Daddy Dog.

One of his puppies is sick.

"Can you take care of
my puppy?"
asks Daddy Dog.

"Yes, I can," says Carl.

Daddy Dog takes
the other puppies out
for a walk.

"How do you feel?" asks Carl.

"I am thirsty," says Puppy.

Carl brings him some water.

"I am hungry," says Puppy.

Carl brings him a snack.

"I am hot," says Puppy.

Carl brings him a fan.

"Now I'm cold," says Puppy.

Carl brings him a blanket.

"I am bored," says Puppy.

Carl brings him a toy.

"I need you to play with me,"
says Puppy.

"No," says Carl.

"What you need is . . .

a good nap."

What's that sound?

It's Daddy Dog and
the other puppies.
They are back from their walk.

"I feel much better now,"
says Puppy.
"Can you take *me* for a walk?"

What a good dog, Carl.